W9-AHJ-833

Colin Thompson

BARRY

RANDOM HOUSE AUSTRALIA

This is Barry.

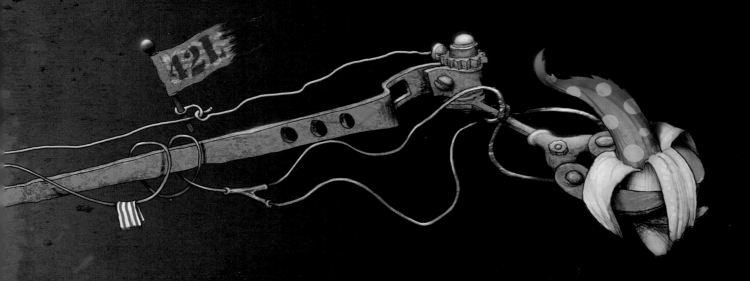

He may look small and insignificant, but size isn't everything.

RULE 6827
Do not stick pins
in balloons.

HUMAN CHILD - SAMPLE 23B

Barry *is* small, but his brain is massive.

Most of it is stored on his home planet far, far away beyond a galaxy that time forgot.

Barry came to Earth in 1952, and got stuck here. He fell down the back of a sofa and none of the aliens who had created him would put their hands between the cushions to get him in case there were cockroaches.

Aliens are terrified of cockroaches so they went home without him.

Barry stayed down the back of the sofa for fifteen years with only an old biscuit, a lipstick and an incredible amount of fluff for company. Lipstick was exactly the same shade of red as the sun back home.

There were no cockroaches because cockroaches are terrified of aliens.

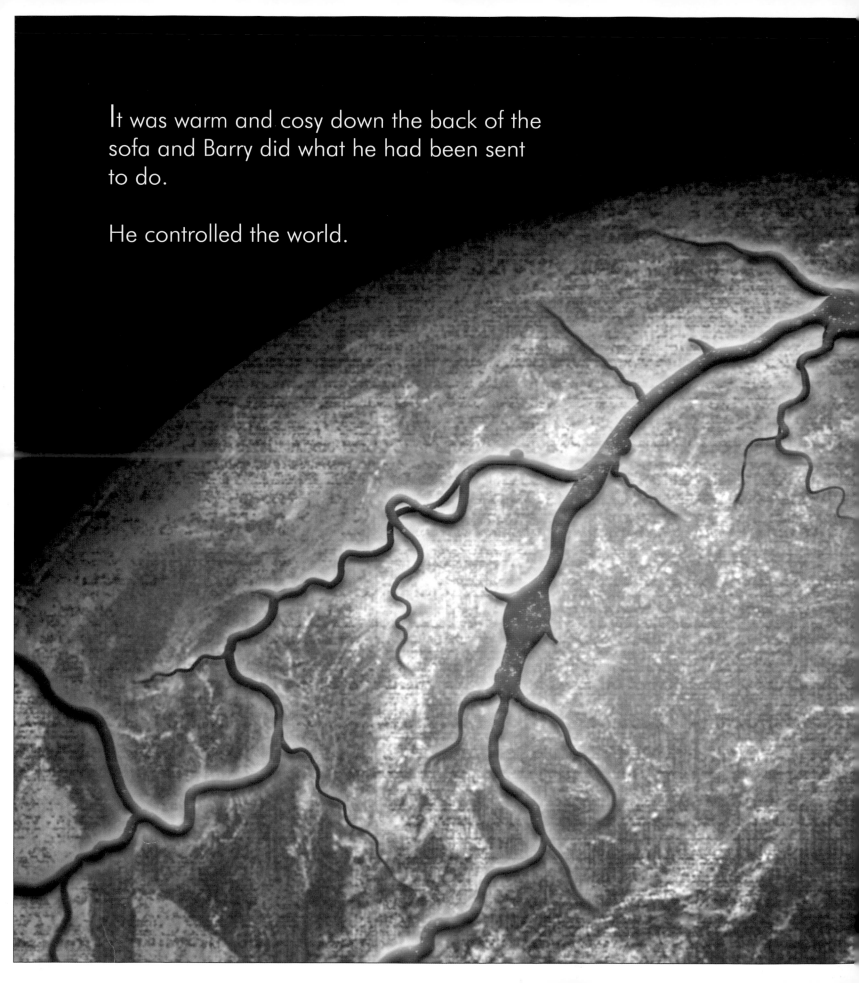

It was warm and cosy down the back of the sofa and Barry did what he had been sent to do.

He controlled the world.

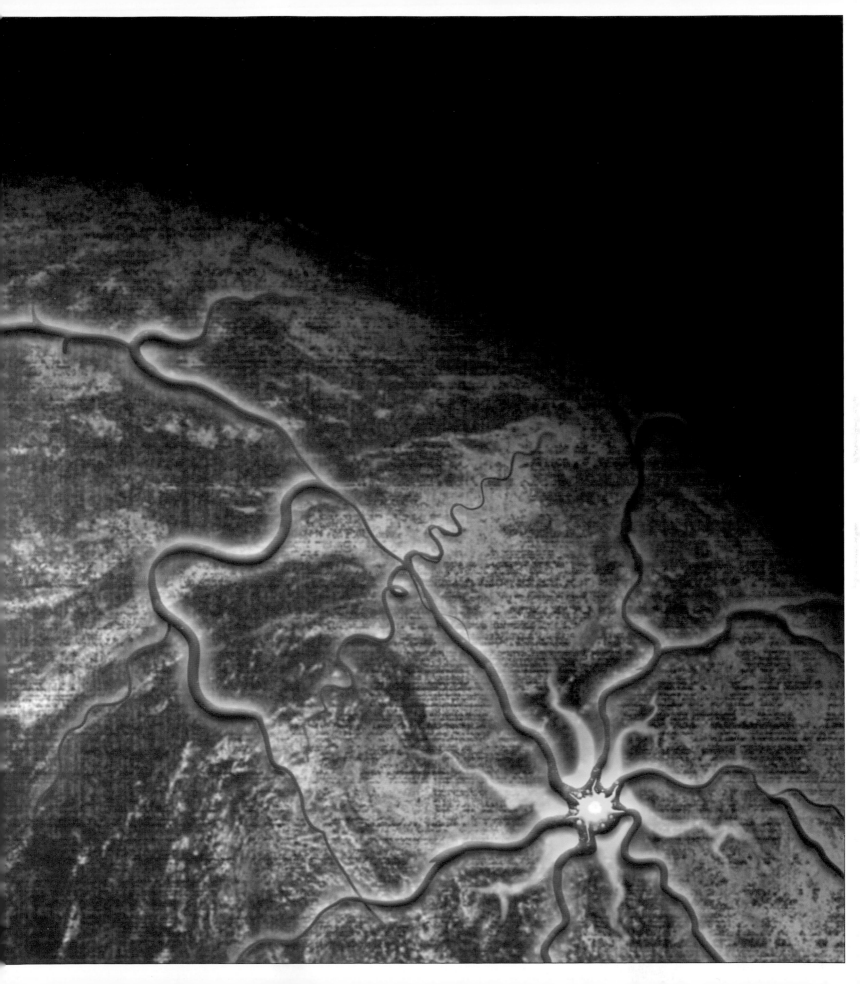

Sun and rain, floods and drought, war and peace, Barry controlled it all and he did it without question. Messages appeared inside his head and told him what to do.

It went on for years, strange distortions of reality that shouldn't really have been happening: the Loch Ness Monster, the Bermuda Triangle, the Abominable Snowman, Bigfoot and *Australia's Got Talent*.

Time passed and a mouse ate the biscuit. The fluff put on a coat of cobwebs and one of Barry's screws became loose. Only Lipstick remained constant.

A year later the screw dropped out and Barry's right arm fell off, but he didn't complain. The mouse had moved his family into the sofa and his children practised biting on Barry's discarded arm. They tried to chew his other arm too and eat Lipstick, but he chased them away with plasma bolts of energy that made their fur stand on end.

Barry never complained, partly because there was no one to complain to and partly because complaining wasn't part of his programming so he didn't know how to do it.

They must know what they're doing, he thought and then he thought, *Hello Lipstick, you're looking nice today.*

Lipstick didn't reply.

A few more years passed and several exciting things happened. A spoon arrived. It fell on Barry's head and covered his good eye. That made the droughts worse, and the floods bigger and all the ice began to melt.

The most exciting thing happened in 1964.

Barry had a visitor. The baby that lived in the house had got bigger and started poking her hand down the back of the sofa. At first Barry ignored the hand, even when it kept taking his fluff and even when it took his fallen off arm. It chewed his leg for a bit and then gave it back to him covered in dribble and pureed carrot.

But when it reached out for Lipstick, Barry took action. He grabbed Lipstick and drew on the back of the baby's hand.

The humans made a lot of noise when the baby pulled her hand out. The lady shouted at the boy who said it wasn't him and to prove it he put his hand down the sofa.

Barry did not draw a kissy mouth on the boy's hand. He wrote a very rude word he had heard the father use.

The humans made even more noise.

Barry went to the quietest corner of the sofa and kept very still.

He charged up his two million megawatt laser, just in case.

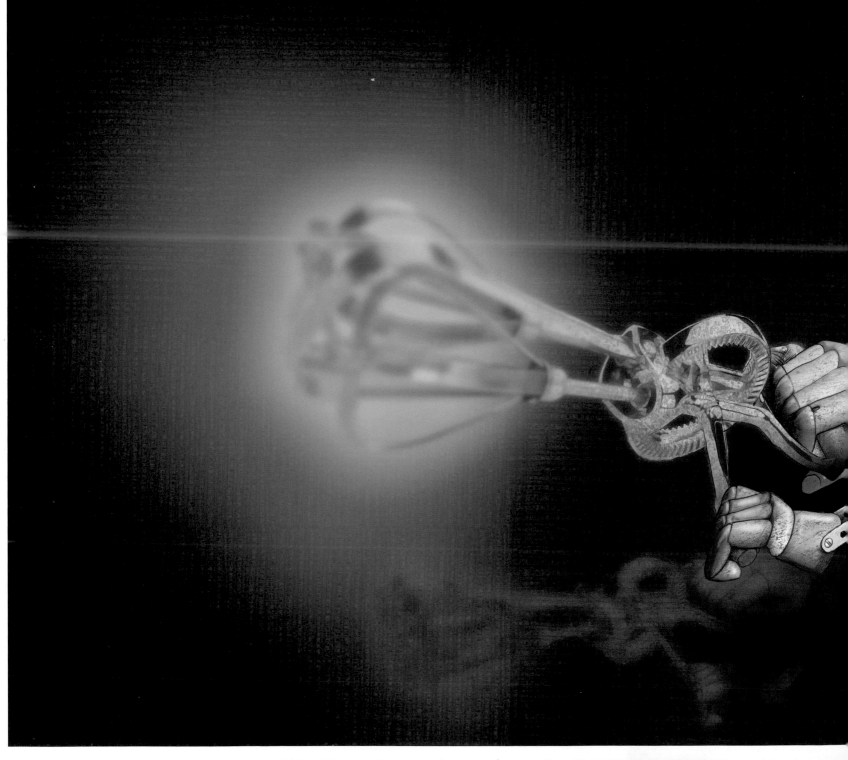

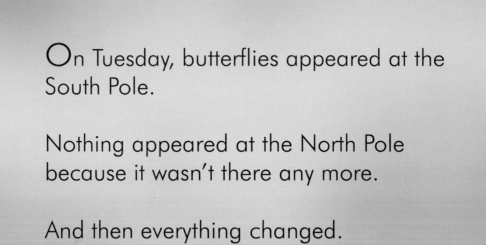

On Tuesday, butterflies appeared at the South Pole.

Nothing appeared at the North Pole because it wasn't there any more.

And then everything changed.

An enormous hand appeared. It picked up the spoon. Then it came back and picked up Barry.

After more than fifty years in the soft darkness inside the sofa, the daylight was deafening and everything else was even louder. The big hand poked him with a screwdriver and a lot of his insides fell out, but he didn't complain. He still controlled the world.

Only it wasn't the same now. From the shelf at the back of the room where he had been put in a plastic box, he could see the television and he knew there were not supposed to be butterflies at the South Pole and nothing where the North Pole had been.

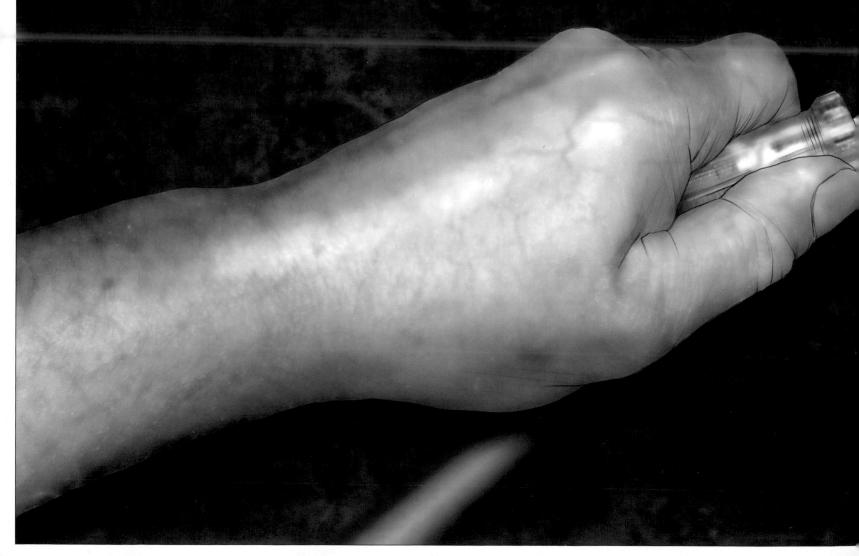

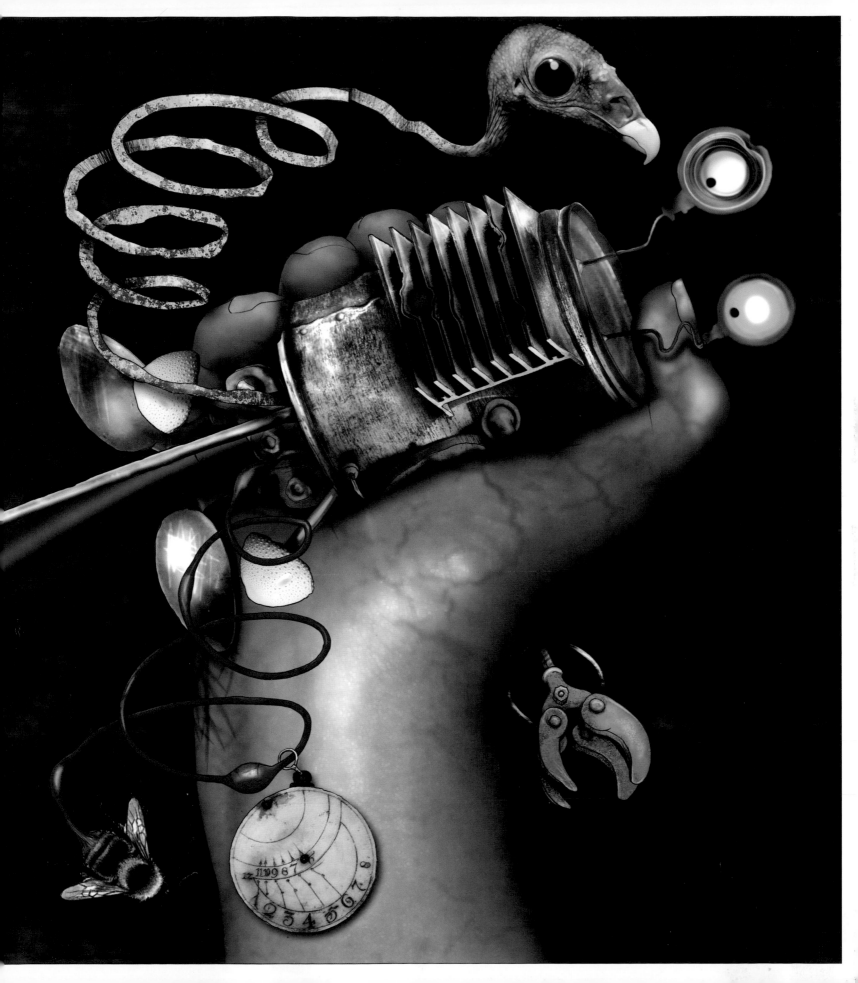

*O*ooops, he thought and reprogrammed himself.

The droughts and the earthquakes got smaller and the floods got smaller too.

Barry went into emergency mode. He sent messages home and got new instructions. Then he began to put everything back how it had been some time before 1952 – give or take twenty thousand years.

They know what they're doing, he thought.

All the droughts and all the deadly diseases and all the bad stuff floating in the air and water and in people's bodies and brains would all soon be fixed.

It was called **Plan B, subsection 14a, *The Massive Ice Age – Cleansing of the Planet Edition*.**

Soon things would be back on track.

After all, Barry thought, as the snow began to bury everything, *it worked last time.*